Poké Rap

I want to be the very best there ever was
To beat all the rest, yeah, that's my cause

Catch 'em, Catch 'em, Gotta catch 'em all

Pokémon I'll search across the land
Look far and wide
Release from my hand
The power that's inside

Catch 'em, Catch 'em, Gotta catch 'em all
Pokémon!

Gotta catch 'em all, Gotta catch 'em all
Gotta catch 'em all, Gotta catch 'em all

At least one hundred and fifty or more to see
To be a Pokémon Master is my destiny

Catch 'em, Catch 'em, Gotta catch 'em all
Gotta catch 'em all, Pokémon! (repeat three times)

Can YOU Rap all 150?
Here's the next 32 Pokémon.

Alakazam, Goldeen, Venonat, Machoke
Kangaskhan, Hypno, Electabuzz, Flareon
Blastoise, Poliwhirl, Oddish, Drowzee
Raichu, Nidoqueen, Bellsprout, Starmie

Metapod, Marowak, Kakuna, Clefairy
Dodrio, Seadra, Vileplume, Krabby
Lickitung, Tauros, Weedle, Nidoran
Machop, Shellder, Porygon, Hitmonchan

There are more books
about Pokémon.

Collect them all!

"*Whooooooooooooooooooh . . .*" The voice was all around them now.

"Help!" Ash, Misty, and Brock all screamed at once. Pikachu jumped into Ash's arms.

From out of nowhere, a Flying Pokémon hopped into the center of the clearing. The Pokémon had a round body, two short wings, and huge red eyes.

Red beams of light poured from the Pokémon's eyes. The light hit the spooky faces on the trees. The faces evaporated

as soon as the light made contact. The mysterious voice died down.

The Flying Pokémon looked at Ash.

"*Hoothoot!*" said the Pokémon.

2

Hoothoot

A dark figure stepped into the clearing. Ash recognized the boy with wavy brown hair and a smug grin on his face.

It was Gary, another Pokémon trainer — Ash's greatest rival.

Gary walked up to the Flying Pokémon and patted it on the head.

"Well done, Hoothoot," Gary said.

Ash rubbed his eyes. "Am I seeing things?" he asked.

"Those faces in the trees were an illusion," Gary said. "But I'm real. And as usual, I'm way ahead of you, Ash."

Ash groaned. That was Gary, all right. He thought he was so much better than Ash.

But what was Gary doing here? And what was the deal with that Hoothoot, anyway?

Ash took out his Pokédex, Dexter. His handheld computer stored information about all kinds of Pokémon.

"Hoothoot, the Owl Pokémon," Dexter said. "It always stands on one leg and can see clearly through even the darkest night."

"You'll never get through this forest without a Hoothoot," Gary said.

"What do you mean?" Ash asked.

"Without a Hoothoot, you'll get lost," Gary said. "You should have known that. But of course you didn't. That's what makes me a winner and you a loser."

Ash felt a familiar anger rise up inside him. "We'll see who does better in the Johto League." In the league, Ash and Gary would compete against other Pokémon trainers to see who was best.

Gary sneered. "You have to get there

first! Come on, Hoothoot."

Gary and the Hoothoot disappeared down one of the trails.

"All we need to do is find a Hoothoot to lead us out," Ash said.

Misty rolled her eyes. "That's not going to be easy to do in the middle of this dark forest," she said.

Ash wasn't ready to give up. "I'll catch one. You'll see!"

An hour later, they were still lost in the woods. There was no sign of a Hoothoot anywhere.

"Hoothoot, where are you?" Ash called for what seemed like the millionth time.

Misty followed behind them. "We're never going to get out of this forest," she complained.

Ash sighed. He brushed a strand of dark hair away from his face. The only reason he was traveling through the strange forest was so he could compete against other trainers in the Johto League and earn badges. It was the only way to become a Pokémon Master.

But now they were lost. Maybe Gary was right. Ash would never even get to the Johto League.

"*Hoot!*"

Ash spun around.

"Did you hear something?" he asked.

"*Hoothoot!*"

"I did it!" Ash cried. "I found a Hoothoot."

Misty looked down at her feet. A Hoothoot looked at Misty adoringly as it nuzzled against her sneakers.

"It looks like this Hoothoot found *me*," Misty corrected Ash.

"We'll see about that," Ash said. "Come here, Hoothoot!"

Hoothoot hopped on one foot to Ash. It hopped onto Ash's head.

Then it started to peck at Ash's skull with its beak.

"Ow!" Ash cried. "Cut it out!"

The Hoothoot jumped down and hopped along the trail.

"Let's follow it," said Misty.

Ash took off after the Hoothoot, rubbing his sore head as he ran. The path grew

wider and wider. Up ahead, Ash saw a stone archway. The Hoothoot ran right through it.

Ash and the others kept up with the Hoothoot. The Flying Pokémon stopped at a large stone pillar carved with an image of a Hoothoot.

"This place is creepier than the forest," Misty said, shivering.

"Who are you calling creepy?" a shrill voice asked.

A short old woman stepped out from behind the pillar. She wore a green skirt, a pink shirt, and a necklace made of chunky blue beads. Deep wrinkles creased her round face.

"It's another illusion!" Ash yelled. "Pikachu, use Thundershock!"

"*Pika?*" Pikachu didn't sound so sure.

The old woman walked up to Ash and sharply pulled his ear.

"Ow!" Ash cried for the second time that night.

"I'm no illusion, young man," she said. "My name is Hagatha. If you want to get out of this forest you'd better follow me."

Ash looked at
Brock and Misty.
They shrugged.
They followed
Hagatha and the
Hoothoot to a
small wooden

cabin. They sat down to talk. Hagatha
closed one eye and studied Ash's face.

"So you're lost, are you?" she finally
asked.

"We *were* lost," Ash said. "Then we found
this Hoothoot. It's going to lead us out of
the forest."

Hagatha's mouth cracked into a smile.
Then she began to laugh.

"This Hoothoot?" she said. "You're new to
these parts, aren't you?"

Ash frowned.

"We are lost," Misty interrupted. "Can
you help us?"

"I rent Hoothoot to travelers who pass
this way," Hagatha explained. "Hoothoot
have the power to see through the illusions
in the forest. They can get you safely

through to the other side."

So this is where Gary got his Hoothoot, Ash thought.

"Perfect!" Misty said. "Can we rent one from you?"

Hagatha shook her head. "That's what I was trying to tell your friend. This Hoothoot here is the only one I have left. It's never made it safely through the forest yet. You're welcome to stay here with me tonight. The other Hoothoot guides will return in the morning."

"Sounds good to me," Misty said, yawning.

"No!" Ash said, jumping up. "Gary will be way ahead of us by then. Can't we just take *this* Hoothoot? I'm a great trainer. I can handle it."

Ash held out a hand to the Hoothoot. The Pokémon ignored him. It hopped onto Misty's lap. It gazed adoringly into her blue eyes. It nuzzled against her orange hair.

Hagatha smiled. "I forgot to mention that this Hoothoot has another weakness," she said. "A weakness for pretty girls."

"*Hoot!*" Hoothoot cuddled up to Misty.

"Pretty girls?" Ash asked. "Where?"

"Hey!" Misty protested.

Ash ignored her. "What do you say, Hagatha?" Ash asked. "Can we take it?"

Hagatha shrugged. "It doesn't look like I can stop you."

"I have one question," Brock said. "About the illusions in the forest. Do you know what causes them?"

Hagatha's blue eyes twinkled. "That, my friends, is something of a mystery."

"A mystery. Cool!" Ash said. "We're great at solving mysteries."

"We'll see," Hagatha said. "Good luck!"

Ash and the others left the small cabin. Hoothoot stood at Misty's feet.

"All right, Hoothoot," Ash said. "Lead the way!"

Hoothoot didn't budge. It looked up at Misty.

"Come on, Hoothoot," Misty said in a sweet voice. "You'll help us, won't you?"

"*Hoothoot!*" The Pokémon began to hop back down the trail.

Ash's spirits lifted as they traveled deeper and deeper into the woods. They'd catch up to Gary in no time.

Suddenly, Hoothoot stopped. It flapped its wings frantically, then turned around and looked at them.

"What's the matter, Hoothoot?" Misty asked.

Hoothoot started to shiver and shake. Ash thought the Pokémon looked terrified.

"Hoothoot, what is it?" Ash asked.

The next instant, many glowing balls of light appeared in the air. The balls were about the size of baseballs and seemed to be surrounded by an eerie blue gas.

"Ash, watch out!" Brock cried.

One of the balls of light swirled through the air, aimed right for Ash's head!

Too Many Ashes

Ash ducked. The ball of light narrowly missed him. The other balls dodged around Misty and Brock.

"They must be illusions," Ash said. "Hoothoot, stop them!"

Hoothoot didn't move.

"Please, Hoothoot!" Misty pleaded.

The many balls of light came together, forming a triangle. Hoothoot aimed its large red eyes at the lights. Ash could see it was trying to make red beams come out of its eyes, like Gary's Hoothoot had done.

It just couldn't do it.

The balls of light started to take shape. They formed a scary mask of blue light. Two hollow eyes stared at them. A huge, gaping mouth moaned.

"*Hoot!*" Hoothoot hopped away from the face as fast as it could.

"*Wahahahahahaha!*" cackled the mask. It dove after Ash and his friends. Ash picked up Pikachu and ran after Hoothoot with Brock and Misty at his heels.

Finally, it looked like the illusion — or whatever it was — had given up. Ash stopped to catch his breath. He set Pikachu down on the ground.

"What happened, Hoothoot?" Ash asked the Flying Pokémon. "Why did you leave us behind?"

"*Hoot?*" Hoothoot didn't seem to think it had done anything wrong.

"What did you expect, Ash?" Misty asked. "Hagatha told us this Hoothoot isn't a good guide. We could be sleeping in a safe place right now. Instead, we're more lost than ever. And something's out to get us!"

"Hagatha said they're just illusions," Ash reminded her. "Illusions can't hurt us, can they?"

At that moment, a rope descended from the sky. The rope twirled around Pikachu, then lifted the Pokémon into the air.

"*Pika!*" Pikachu cried.

"Ash, I don't think that's an illusion," Brock said.

Ash jumped up and grabbed onto the end of the rope. He hung on as best as he could while the rope rose higher and higher.

Ash had a sinking feeling he knew what he would hear next.

"Prepare for trouble!" said a girl's voice.

"Make it double!" added a boy's voice.

Ash looked up. It was Team Rocket, a trio of Pokémon thieves. Jessie, James, and the Pokémon, Meowth, were always trying to steal Pikachu. This time, Jessie and James were perched in the top branches of a tall tree, holding on to a giant fishing pole. The rope dangled from the end of the pole. They were reeling in the rope like a fishing line. But instead of a fish, they had nabbed Ash and Pikachu.

Jessie smiled an evil smile. "Well, hello, twerp," she called down. "We didn't expect to see you hanging around here."

"But since you're here, we might as well steal your Pikachu," added James.

Meowth, the scratch cat Pokémon, grinned. "And now you're in for a *tree*-mendous surprise," Meowth said.

"*Tree*-mendous?" Ash asked. "What are you — whoaaaaa!"

Jessie and James swung the fishing rod sharply to the side. Ash slammed face first into a sturdy tree trunk. The crash caused him to loosen his grip. He slid down the trunk to the forest floor.

"*Pika!*" Pikachu cried. Jessie and James quickly reeled in the little Pokémon. James held up the rope as Pikachu dangled in front of him.

"That's what I call a great catch," Jessie said triumphantly.

Meowth opened the lid of a square box. "This electric-proof Pika-prison will prevent any shocking surprises from Pikachu," Meowth said. James dropped Pikachu into the box, and Meowth snapped the lid shut.

"Hey, give me back my Pikachu!" Ash yelled up at them.

"If we handed it over that easily, we wouldn't be doing our jobs, would we?" Jessie pointed out.

"And now it's time for our great escape!" James announced.

The blue-haired boy pushed aside a tree branch to reveal a small row-boat hanging from two ropes. The ropes stretched across the forest. Ash saw that the boat was attached to the ropes with two pulleys.

Jessie, James, and Meowth jumped into the boat. Meowth carried the box that held Pikachu.

"We've finally done it!" Meowth said. "The Boss isn't going to believe it."

"Time to shove off," James said. He pulled a lever, and the boat moved along the

ropes, away
from the
tree.

Jessie
waved good-
bye. "You'll
never see
Pikachu
ag —
aaaaaaaaaaaaah!"

The ropes supporting the boat snapped in half. The boat crashed to the forest floor. The lid to the box popped open, and Pikachu dashed away and jumped into Ash's arms.

"Pikachu!" Ash cried, hugging his Pokémon.

"This isn't over yet," Jessie said, brushing leaves from her white Team Rocket uniform. "We're not leaving without a fight." She held out a red-and-white Poké Ball.

"I'm always ready for a battle," Ash replied. He took a Poké Ball from his belt.

"You're up, Arbok!" Jessie cried, throwing the ball. A purple Pokémon that looked like a snake appeared in a flash of light.

"Come on out, Victreebel!" yelled James. He threw a Poké Ball, and out popped a Pokémon that looked like a giant plant. Victreebel had a large yellow flower bell for a body. As usual, the bell swallowed James in one gulp.

"How many times do I have to tell you?" James screamed, his legs kicking in the air. "Attack them, not me!"

Ash threw a Poké Ball. Beating these

clowns would be easy.

"Bulbasaur, I choose you!" Ash cried.

A white light flashed, and a Grass Pokémon appeared. Bulbasaur looked like a small dinosaur with a plant bulb on its back.

Ash tensed.

Hoothoot made the first move. The Flying Pokémon ran in front of Ash. It hopped around nervously, flapping its wings.

Team Rocket saw a large orange Pokémon in the distance.

"A Dragonite!" Meowth cried.

"That rare Pokémon is a more precious prize than Pikachu," Jessie said.

"We've got to catch it," James said. "Come on, Victreebel."

Jessie, James, and Meowth ran off after the Dragonite. Victreebel and Arbok followed.

"Something tells me Team Rocket saw an illusion," Brock said, stepping in front of Ash.

"I don't care if it's an illusion," Ash said. "I'm just glad it got rid of Team Rocket. Right, Pikachu?"

Ash looked down at his little Pokémon. Pikachu looked terrified.

"What's the matter, Pikachu?" Ash asked. Then he noticed his friends. Brock and Misty had both turned pale. Togepi covered its eyes with its tiny arms.

"What's wrong?" Ash asked. His voice echoed strangely.

Ash slowly turned around.

He was surrounded by exact copies of himself!

"It can't be," Ash cried. "There's only one Ash. And it's me!"

4

Ghostly Illusions

Ash knew the copies of himself had to be illusions. But they seemed so real.

Dozens of clones surrounded Ash.

"Ash, which one is the real you?" Misty called out.

"I'm right here!" Ash cried. But the copies all spoke out at the same time, drowning his voice.

"No, I'm the real Ash!"

"It's me!"

"No, he's a fake!"

"Don't let them trick you! I'm the one!"

Ash waved his arms, trying to make himself look different from the others. He jumped up and down. It didn't work. The copies all did the same.

Misty knelt down beside Pikachu. "Can you tell which is the real Ash?" she asked.

"It's me, Pikachu. I'm here!" Ash cried, but the copies all did the same.

Pikachu looked at the crowd of Ashes, confused.

The Ash copies all gathered around Pikachu.

"I'm the real one, Pikachu!"

"Tell them, Pikachu."

"It's me, Pikachu. Can't you see?"

Ash could see that Pikachu was trying to focus, trying to find him, but it was too confused. Pikachu held its head in its hands.

Then Pikachu did what it knew how to do best.

"*Pikachuuuuuuuuuuuuuuuuuuu!*" Lightning flashed as Pikachu aimed a sizzling electric charge at the copies.

Ash braced himself as the attack sizzled his body. The copies disappeared as soon as the electricity hit them, leaving Ash standing alone — and more than a little frazzled.

"Good work, Pikachu," Ash said weakly. He patted the yellow Pokémon on the head.

"*Eeeeeeeeeeeeeeeeek!*" A high-pitched scream pierced the night air.

Ash spun around. Misty was surrounded by Bug Pokémon.

"Help me!" Misty yelled.

Ash knew Misty hated Bug Pokémon. And now some of the creepiest Bug

30

Pokémon were all around her. Venomoth flapped its wings above her head. Beedrill buzzed next to her ear. Caterpie and Weedle inched toward her. Metapod stared at her with its big eyes.

"It's just an illusion, Misty," Ash reminded her. "They can't hurt you!"

"They look pretty real to me," Misty said. "Where's Hoothoot? Maybe it can get rid of these things."

Ash turned to the Flying Pokémon.

Hoothoot was hopping away as fast as it could.

"Wait, Hoothoot!" Ash called out.

Hoothoot kept hopping.

"You can't abandon Misty," Ash said, running after it. "She needs you."

Hoothoot stopped and turned around.

"You're the only one who can save Misty," Ash said. "You can do it. I know you can."

Hoothoot turned and faced the swarm of Bug Pokémon. Ash could see it was concentrating with all its might.

"This illusion is really bugging me!"

Misty said. "Please help, Hoothoot."

Hoothoot's round eyes began to glow with red light — just like the eyes of Gary's Pokémon had done.

The red lights got stronger and stronger. They formed a powerful beam that shot out and hit the Bug Pokémon. The creepy creatures faded away until there was nothing left.

Misty sighed with relief. "Thanks, Hoothoot," she said.

Hoothoot looks strong and confident now, Ash thought. Next the Flying Pokémon aimed the red eye beams at the trees in the forest.

Ash gasped. The red light revealed hordes of Ghost Pokémon hiding in the treetops. Gray-purple Haunter with creepy claws. Gengar with spooky orange eyes.

"There are tons of them," Ash said, amazed.

"Ah-ha!" Brock exclaimed. "So the Ghost Pokémon were creating the illusions all along."

"I think I've had enough illusions for one

night," Ash said. He turned to Bulbasaur. "Use your Vine Whip!"

Two long green vines lashed out of the plant bulb on Bulbasaur's back. The vines shot up into the trees and knocked the Ghost Pokémon off the branches.

"Pikachu, Thunderbolt!" Ash yelled.

Red sparks crackled on Pikachu's cheeks as it charged up for the attack. Then Pikachu hurled a blast of electric energy at the falling Ghost Pokémon. The attack sent the Haunter and Gengar flying deep into the forest.

"We did it!" Ash cheered. "It must have been my training that got Hoothoot to help us. Right, Hoothoot?"

Hoothoot jumped on Ash's head and pecked away with its sharp beak.

Misty laughed. "You didn't train it, Ash. Hoothoot just wanted to help me. Right, Hoothoot?"

Hoothoot smiled. It jumped off Ash's head and hopped into Misty's arms.

Ash frowned. "Well, at least we solved the mystery of the illusions."

"Actually, Ash, that was Hoothoot, too," Brock said. "It was Hoothoot's ability to see through the illusions that showed us the truth."

"Oh, yeah," Ash admitted. He walked over to Hoothoot.

"You've been a big help, Hoothoot," Ash said. "How about getting us safely through the forest now?"

Hoothoot looked up at Misty.

"Do it for all of us, Hoothoot," Misty said. "You're a real guide now."

Hoothoot nodded and hopped to the ground.

"*Hoothoot!*"

5

Caught in Spinarak's Web

"I'm glad we finally made it out of that forest," Ash said the next day. "Hoothoot was a huge help. Too bad we had to say good-bye." It had only taken Hoothoot another hour to get them to safety. They even had time to sleep for a while. Ash felt refreshed — and ready for anything.

"I'm glad we're headed for Cattailia City," Misty added. "It'll be a relief to see concrete and buildings instead of a bunch of spooky trees."

Soon the friends reached the town. The

streets were lined with old brick buildings. Ash thought the whole place seemed kind of peaceful.

"This looks like a great place for a rest," Brock said, sitting down on a wooden bench. "Facing those illusions was draining."

Just then, a police car zoomed by, its sirens blaring. Brock jumped to his feet.

"Where there's a police car, there's bound to be Officer Jenny," Brock said. He raced down the sidewalk.

Ash and Misty looked at each other. Each town had an Officer Jenny. They all

looked alike, and they were all related. And Brock had a crush on every one of them.

"Brock is so girl crazy," Ash remarked, making a face. "I hope I'm never that bad."

"You'd better not be," Misty said, "because no girl would be crazy enough to like you."

"Hey!" Ash said.

"We'd better go after him," said Misty. She ran after Brock.

Ash and Misty caught up to Brock just in time to see him trip. He fell headfirst into the concrete.

"Are you okay, Brock?" Misty asked. She leaned over her friend. Suddenly, Togepi started waving its arms and pointing.

"*Togi! Togi!*" said the Pokémon frantically.

"What's the matter, Togepi?" Misty asked. She looked up.

Something had dropped down from the sky. It looked like a round frowning face attached to a string.

"Hey, what's this?" Misty said, smiling. She reached out to touch it.

The frowning face spun around. Ash could see that there was a head and six legs attached to it.

"A b-b-b-b-b-bug!" Misty yelled. She jumped back.

It was too late. The Bug Pokémon shot a strand of sticky string out of its spinneret. The string wrapped around Ash, Misty, Brock, and Pikachu. They were stuck in the sticky trap.

"This is what I call a sticky situation," Ash joked.

"That's not funny, Ash," said Misty. "We're trapped by that horrible bug!"

Ash studied the Pokémon. It had a green head and body. What Ash thought was a frowning face were actually black marks on the Pokémon's body. Its legs were yellow and black. It had a tiny white horn on top of its head.

"I think it's kind of cute," Ash said.

"Yuck!" Misty made a face.

Brock made a face, too. He got a dreamy look in his eyes. "Officer Jenny," Brock said.

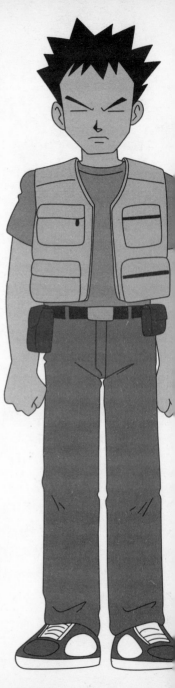

A pretty police officer with blue hair approached them. She was flanked by two male officers in blue uniforms.

"It looks like Spinarak caught the thieves," said one of the men.

Officer Jenny frowned. "Do these kids really look like master thieves to you?" she asked.

"We're not thieves," Ash said quickly. "We're Pokémon trainers."

"I believe you, but I'd still like to ask you some questions," Jenny said. She turned to the officers. "Get them out of that web."

A while later, Ash, Brock, Misty, and Pikachu faced Officer Jenny across a round table at the police station.

"Sorry you got stuck in that web," Jenny said. "We hung them to catch a thief who's been striking the town. The thief is imitating the famous jewel thief, The Black Arachnid."

"The Black Arachnid?" Ash asked. "That name sounds familiar."

"The Black Arachnid was a master thief

who traveled all over the world," Jenny said. "His partner was a Meowth. The Pokémon would use an attack called Pay Day to scare away anyone who tried to catch them."

"Pay Day," Brock said. "I've heard of that. The Pokémon can make a shower of coins appear out of thin air, right?"

Jenny nodded. "Right. That's how we know that this new thief is a The Black Arachnid imitator." She held out a shiny object. It looked like a silver coin with the words *Pay Day* written on it.

"The new thief is using Pay Day, too," she explained.

"So how does that Bug Pokémon fit in?" Ash asked.

Jenny looked at her Spinarak and beamed with pride. "My great-grand-mother, Officer Jenny, caught the first Black Arachnid. Her Spinarak spun a web and trapped him and his Meowth. It was beautiful."

"I see," Brock said. "So now you want to use Spinarak to trap the The Black

Arachnid imitator."

"Exactly!" Officer Jenny said. "I hope we catch him soon. I'd like to know who this imitator is. It's a real mystery!"

Ash perked up. "A mystery!" he said. "Then you're lucky you found us. We'll help you solve this mystery in no time."

Setting a Trap

"You solve mysteries, huh?" Officer Jenny looked from Ash to Brock to Misty. She eyed Pikachu and Togepi.

"No, it couldn't be," she muttered. She walked to a desk and picked up a piece of paper.

"My sister in New Bark Town sent me a letter about a group of kids who helped her find a missing Totodile," Jenny said. "They called themselves Pokémon burglary investigators. Was she talking about you?"

Brock jumped up.

"That's us! Pokémon bur-
glary investigators, at your
service," he said.

Ash didn't stop
Brock. After all, they
had helped the Officer
Jenny in New Bark Town
get Totodile back. They might
not be official Pokémon burglary investigators, but he had
to admit he liked the sound
of it.

"We'll help you trap The
Black Arachnid," Ash said.
"Right, Misty?"

Misty shrugged. "Why not?
It might be — aaaaaaaaaaaah!"

A Spinarak dropped down
from the ceiling. It landed on
Officer Jenny's shoulder.

Misty pushed her chair
back. Ash took a closer look
at the Spinarak.

"That sure is a cool-looking
Pokémon," Ash said. He took

Dexter out of his pocket.

"Spinarak, the String Spit Pokémon," Dexter said. "It uses spin-nerets on both its mouth and rear to build webs. Then it waits for its prey. It is able to climb any surface freely."

"I thought you'd be using Growlithe," Brock said. "The officers in all the other towns do."

"Ever since my great-grandmother used a Spinarak to trap The Black Arachnid, we've been using them here," Jenny replied. "They haven't let us down yet."

A uniformed officer ran into the room. His face was flushed with excitement, and he waved a piece of paper in one hand.

"Bad news, Officer Jenny," said the offi-cer. "We just received a letter from the thief. It describes his next crime."

Jenny read the letter. "The Black Arachnid copycat says he'll strike at mid-night tonight. He plans to steal a rare silver trophy."

"Okay, everybody," said Ash. "Let's go!"

They all went to the home of the rich old man who owned the silver trophy. Tall trees bordered the house in back. The green

46

lawns and gardens around the house were perfectly groomed. The blue water of a swimming pool sparkled in the setting sun. Ash marveled at the stone statues of Pokémon that decorated the lawn.

A butler led them inside the house. A short, round man with gray hair approached them. He was nervously wringing his hands.

"You must help me," said the rich old man. "The silver trophy is my most prized possession."

"Can you take us to it?" Jenny asked.

The rich old man nodded. He walked down a hallway and opened a door.

Ash gasped. The room was filled with statues and figures of Pokémon made out of crystal, glass, and marble. In the center of the room, a silver cup sat on a round platform. The handle of the cup was shaped like a Dragonair, a sleek Water Pokémon.

"It's beautiful," Ash said. He turned to the rich old man. "Don't worry, sir. We won't let anything happen to it."

The rich old man gave Jenny a strange

look. "Who are these kids?"

"We're Pokémon burglary investigators," Ash said. He liked the sound of that more and more. "You may have heard of our adventures in New Bark Town."

The rich old man didn't look any happier.

"Don't worry, sir," Officer Jenny told him. "Spinarak and I will oversee everything. We won't let The Black Arachnid succeed."

The rich old man nodded. "I trust you."

Ash turned to his friends. "All right! Let's get started."

Ash walked outside the mansion as the others followed. He threw four Poké Balls into the air.

Charizard, a combination Flying and Fire Pokémon, came out and stomped its large feet on the ground. It flapped its strong wings.

Then came Squirtle, a Water Pokémon that looked like a cute turtle.

Heracross popped out next. This blue Bug Pokémon was as tall as Ash. Ash had caught Heracross just a few weeks ago, but it had already helped him out of some tough situations.

Bulbasaur appeared. Heracross flew over to it and started to suck the sweet nectar from Bulbasaur's plant bulb. Bulbasaur quickly shrugged off the Bug Pokémon.

"Wow, you have a lot of different types of Pokémon," Jenny said, impressed. "I guess I shouldn't expect less from professional burglary investigators."

Misty rolled her eyes. "This is going a little too far," she muttered under her breath.

Ash turned to his Pokémon.

"All right, guys," he said. "Bulbasaur, you hide in the garden."

Bulbasaur obeyed. Its blue-green body blended perfectly with all of the plants and flowers.

"Heracross, wait back by those trees," Ash said next.

Hercross flew to the wooded area. Its blue body acted as camouflage against the tree trunks.

"Squirtle, into the pool," Ash told the Water Pokémon.

Squirtle jumped into the pool and hid under the water.

Ash looked around the grounds. Hiding Charizard wouldn't be so easy. Then he had an idea.

"Charizard, stand over by those statues," Ash said. "Try, uh, to blend in."

Charizard struck a pose next to a statue of a Blastoise.

Ash turned to Officer Jenny. "All of our Pokémon are in place," he said.

"Okay, Spinarak," Jenny told the Bug

Pokémon. "Do your thing!"

Spinarak jumped off Jenny's shoulder. It crawled up the side of the mansion.

"We'd better get inside," Jenny said. They followed her to the doorway.

A nearly invisible string of sticky webbing came out of Spinarak's two spinnerets. Ash watched in amazement as Spinarak quickly spun a web over the entire mansion. The web stretched out over the lawns, all the way to the stone walls that protected the estate.

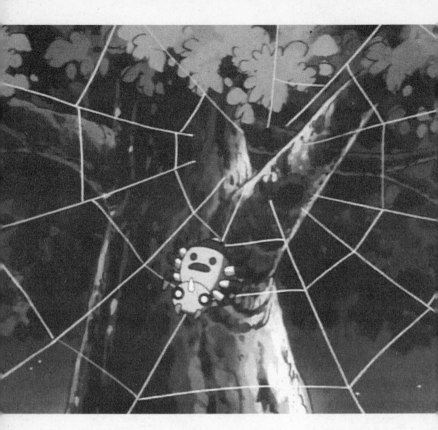

"We should catch the thief no matter which way he tries to get in," Officer Jenny said. "Spinarak's web is incredibly strong. Anyone who gets caught in it can't move at all."

"We know," Misty said, remembering how they had gotten trapped earlier.

"So what do we do now?" Ash asked.

"We wait," Officer Jenny said.

Ash and Pikachu stood guard by the front door. Misty, Brock, and Officer Jenny waited by other doors and windows. The rich old man stayed in the Pokémon room. He wanted to guard the Dragonair cup himself.

Time seemed to pass slowly. Ash yawned, trying to stay awake. He slumped to the floor. Pikachu was already napping at his feet.

After what seemed like days, a clock in the hallway chimed twelve times.

"It's midnight!" Ash yelled, jumping up. "Pikachu, wake up."

Pikachu opened its eyes as Officer Jenny, Misty, and Brock joined them.

"Any sign of the thief?" Ash asked.

"No," Officer Jenny replied. "Spinarak's nets haven't been touched. I think we may have scared the thief away."

The rich old man walked into the hall. "The silver cup is still there," he said. "So the The Black Arachnid copycat didn't come. Thank goodness."

Ash beamed. "What do you expect from professional Pokémon burglary investigators?"

Suddenly, a shrill voice rang through the house.

"Pay Day! Pay Day!" yelled the voice.

7

Tricked by Team Rocket?

A panel in the ceiling slid to the side. A shower of silver coins tumbled out.

"It's The Black Arachnid!" Officer Jenny cried.

Two people dressed in black and a Pokémon descended from the ceiling on a rope. There was a girl with long red hair and a boy with blue hair. The Pokémon was a white scratch cat Pokémon — a Meowth.

Ash couldn't believe it.

"Team Rocket?" he said.

Jessie grinned. "I see you didn't expect

us to drop in!" she said.

"How did you get in here?" Ash asked.

James pointed up. "We've been hiding out in the attic since we left the warning letter."

"In other words," Jessie said, "we outwitted you!"

"That explains why they didn't get caught in any of the traps," said Officer Jenny.

Something still didn't make sense to Ash. "Then how come you didn't come until after midnight?"

Jessie, James, and Meowth looked sheepishly at one another.

"We fell asleep," Meowth admitted.

Pikachu jumped up on a table. It started to charge up for an attack.

Meowth didn't look worried. "We don't have time to play right now," Meowth said. "It's time for Pay Day!"

Ash waited for the shower of coins. Nothing happened.

Meowth swatted at James. "Come on, throw them," it whispered.

"Please don't make me," James pleaded.

Jessie bopped James on the head. "You're acting like a master wimp, not a master thief. Just do it!"

James reached into his pocket. Then he tossed a bunch of coins down below.

Ash held up his hands to protect himself from the attack. He saw Misty reach down and pick up one of the objects.

"Hey, these are just bottle caps!" she said.

"They're my prized collection," James called out. "Give them back later, okay?"

Ash laughed. "You guys are pathetic The Black Arachnid imitators. You slept late. And your Meowth doesn't even know the Pay Day attack. You have to fake it."

"Well, we didn't fake this," Jessie said. She held out the silver Dragonair cup.

"No! It can't be!" cried Mr. Miser.

Jessie waved good-bye. "You may call yourself burglary investigators, but you're nothing but a bunch of bunglers. So long!"

Team Rocket disappeared back into the ceiling.

"The roof!" Ash cried. "I bet they've got their balloon."

Ash ran outside, and the others followed.

Team Rocket had climbed into their balloon, all right. But the balloon wasn't going anywhere. Ash saw the Spinarak at work, quickly spinning a web around the basket.

They can't get out of Spinarak's web," Ash said happily.

"History repeats itself," said Officer Jenny. "Anyone using the name The Black Arachnid in this town is destined to be caught by Spinarak."

Team Rocket wasn't giving up. They held up large hand fans and started fanning with all their might.

They created enough of a wind to get the balloon moving a little. Ash sprang into action.

"Squirtle! Bulbasaur! Heracross! Charizard!" he called out. "I need you now!"

Ash's Pokémon came out of their hiding places.

"Squirtle! Water Gun!"

A blast of water exploded from Squirtle's mouth, knocking the fans out of Team Rocket's hands.

"Bulbasaur, Razor Leaf!"

Sharp leaves flew out of Bulbasaur's plant bulb. The leaves sliced through the fabric of Team Rocket's balloon.

"All right, Charizard," Ash said. "Now!"

Charizard shot a stream of hot flame at the web surrounding Team Rocket's balloon. The web disintegrated, and the balloon rose up. But the hole in the balloon was leaking too much air, and the balloon spiraled crazily in the sky.

"Hey, my silver Dragonair cup!" Mr. Miser called out.

Ash cringed. He was used to having his Pokémon blast Team Rocket into the sky. He'd forgotten all about the silver cup.

Officer Jenny called up to Spinarak. "Help us!"

Spinarak aimed a sticky thread at the balloon basket. The thread caught onto the bottom of the basket, pulling the balloon toward the ground.

"We're falling!" Jessie screamed.

Charizard flew up and caught the basket

in its arms. The lizard Pokémon tipped over the basket and started shaking it.

Bottlecaps rained down on the grass.

"My collection!" James yelled.

Then crystal vases, shiny silverware, and other treasures fell from the basket.

"We're losing our loot!" Meowth cried.

"Those are the other treasures they've stolen since they came to our town," Officer Jenny remarked.

Pikachu, Bulbasaur, Squirtle, and Heracross ran around the lawn, catching the treasures as they fell.

The last thing to fall was the silver Dragonair cup.

"I've got it!" Ash yelled. He dove across the grass.

The chalice bounced off Ash's back and landed in Officer Jenny's arms.

"We got it!" Jenny said.

Charizard shook the balloon basket one last time. Jessie, James, and Meowth went flying across the sky.

"Looks like Team Rocket's blasting off again!" they cried.

Officer Jenny handed the cup to Mr. Miser.

"I guess you kids really are professionals," Mr. Miser said. "I can't thank you enough."

"No problem," said Ash. "That's what professional Pokémon burglary investigators do."

"I think Spinarak really saved the day," Misty said. "It's pretty cool — for a Bug Pokémon."

Spinarak landed on Officer Jenny's shoulder.

"You're right about Spinarak," Jenny said. "But I couldn't have done it without you guys."

Brock rushed in front of Jenny. "We did a good job of helping you solve the mystery of The Black Arachnid imitator. Is there anything else we can help you with?"

Ash stepped in front of him. "Sorry, Brock, but we can't stay. I've got to keep moving if I'm going to win any badges."

Brock looked sad at the thought of leaving Officer Jenny.

Misty patted his arm. "Don't worry, Brock. Things are pretty mysterious out here in the west. I bet we'll be helping out another Officer Jenny before you know it."

8

Little Lost Stantler

"There's a big city up ahead," Ash said. "All right! We're getting closer and closer to Violet Town, and the first gym in the Johto League. I can't wait to get another badge."

"Don't forget, you have to beat the Gym Leader first," Misty teased.

"Or maybe we'll have to help Officer Jenny solve another mystery," Brock said. He had a dreamy look in his eyes.

The path they were walking on opened up. A busy metropolis stretched out in front of them. A huge green park sat in the center of the town, surrounded by small buildings and colorful houses.

"This place looks pretty normal to me," Ash remarked. "I can't imagine anything mysterious happening here."

Misty looked at a map. "We have to cross through that park to get to the Pokémon Center."

"Fine with me," Ash said. He took off down the trail with Pikachu at his heels.

Leafy green trees bordered the path through the park. Ash could hear wild Pidgey calling to one another up in the treetops.

"What a peaceful place," Ash said. "Don't you think so, Pikachu?"

"*Pika!*" Pikachu didn't look peaceful at all. The little yellow Pokémon had a look of alarm on its face. It hopped onto Ash's shoulder and pointed to a spot across the path.

"Is something there?" Ash asked. He scanned the leafy border. Then he saw it. Two huge eyes were staring out from the leaves.

"Are those giant eyeballs?" Misty asked.

Brock squinted at them. "I don't think so. Take a closer look."

The eyeballs rustled the leaves. Now Ash could see that what looked like eyeballs were actually two Pokémon antlers with two prongs each. Inside each set of prongs were round balls that looked like pupils.

"I guess they're antlers," Ash said, "but what are they attached to?"

The leaves rustled again. A head poked out.

"Wow, what's that?" Ash wondered. He took out Dexter. A picture of a Pokémon that looked like a deer popped up on the screen.

"Stantler, the Big Horn Pokémon," Dexter said. "The pleasant odor coming from the eyelike shapes at the base of its antlers has a bewildering effect on any who smell it. Stantler generally form herds and live in mountainous terrain."

"I wonder what it's doing here in the

town park," Misty said.

Brock took a step closer. "This one looks like a Stantler," he said. He looked thoughtful. "Let's see . . . when approaching a Pokémon, it's best to imitate the Pokémon's behavior so as not to startle it."

Ash watched as Brock got down on his knees and started to crawl toward the Stantler. He knew his friend wanted to be a great Pokémon breeder. That meant being able to communicate with Pokémon and understand their needs. He wondered if Brock would be successful this time.

Soon Brock and the Stantler were almost nose to nose.

"That's it," Brock said in a soothing voice. "Good little Stantler."

Brock reached out a hand to pet the Stantler's neck. The Stantler stepped back a little. It made a soft, whining sound.

Brock examined the Stantler closely.

"It looks like it's hurt," Brock told the others. "It has a small wound on its knee. If I can get it to trust me, I can help it."

Brock carefully took a small piece of

Pokémon food from his pocket. It was his own special recipe.

"Eat up," he told the Stantler.

The little Stantler sniffed the food, but it didn't take a bite.

Brock bit into it himself. "Mmmm. This is good."

Suddenly, Ash noticed a strange white vapor coming from the Stantler's antlers. The vapor traveled across the path and passed over their heads. Brock didn't seem to see it, though.

Then Ash noticed something else. Something had appeared behind the little Stantler.

It was a whole herd of adult Stantler! They pawed at the ground angrily.

Misty noticed it, too. She hugged Togepi tightly to her.

"Uh, Brock," Ash whispered.

"Not now, Ash," Brock said.

"Brock, look up!" Ash insisted.

Brock raised his head. He froze. Then he slowly stood up.

"Uh, guys," he said. "It looks like they're going to . . ."

"Stampede!" Ash yelled as the Stantler herd charged at them.

9

Stantler Stampede!

Instinct kicked in. Ash picked up Pikachu. Then he turned and ran as fast as he could.

The stampeding Stantler sounded like a thunderstorm as their hooves pounded on the path. If the herd caught up, Ash knew they'd be crushed for sure.

From the corner of his eye, he saw Misty and Brock keeping pace with him.

"We can't outrun them!" Brock yelled over the noise.

"Maybe we can lose them," Misty said.

It seemed hopeless. Ash thought he could feel the Stantler's hot breath on the back of his neck. . . .

And then, suddenly, the thundering noise stopped.

Ash kept running. Finally, when he was sure it was safe, he stopped and looked back.

The path was clear. The herd was nowhere in sight.

"We're safe," Ash said, panting. "The Stantler herd stopped stampeding."

Brock gazed down the path. "That was strange. What happened to that hurt little Stantler? And where could such a huge herd have gone?"

"That's what I'd like to know," a voice said.

Ash, Brock, and Misty turned. It was Officer Jenny.

"I heard you say you saw a Stantler stampede," Jenny said. "All week, I've had reports of a herd of Stantler scaring people in the park. But we can't seem to find them anywhere."

72

"That sounds like a mystery to me," Ash said.

Brock pushed his way in front of Officer Jenny. "We can help you find that Stantler herd. We're professional Pokémon mystery solvers."

"I thought we were Pokémon burglary investigators," Misty muttered.

Brock nudged Misty. He looked at Officer Jenny. "What do you say? Can we help you?"

Officer Jenny looked thoughtful. "Well, I do need you to come down to the station with me so I can file a report. Let's start with that."

Ash and the others followed Officer Jenny to the police station.

At the station, Officer Jenny told them about the Stantler attacks.

"That park is usually full of vacationing families," she explained, "but the Stantler have been scaring them away."

"I thought Stantler lived in the mountains," Misty said. "What are they doing in a park?"

"It's very puzzling," Officer Jenny said.

Brock nodded. "It sure is. The park doesn't look big enough to support a herd of Stantler. And I didn't see any signs that Stantler had been feeding on the plants there."

"That's right," Ash said. "Brock, it sounds like you have an idea about what's happening."

"I might," Brock said thoughtfully.

"Heeeeeeeeeeeeeeelp!" Loud screams came from outside.

Ash and the others followed Officer Jenny as she rushed out to investigate. Ash couldn't believe what they found.

Jessie, James, and Meowth were running down the street, screaming loudly. When they spotted Officer Jenny, they skidded to a stop.

"Help us!" Jessie pleaded. "There's a herd of Stantler chasing us!"

"Those must be the Stantler we just saw," said Misty.

Brock looked down the street. "Where are they?"

"They're right behind us!" James said. "We've got to get inside."

But the street was calm and quiet. There wasn't a Stantler in sight.

"They were here just a minute ago," Meowth said. Then it pointed. "Look. There's one now!" The small Stantler from the park came limping down the street.

"Let's get it and take it to the Boss!" Jessie cried. She held out a Poké Ball.

Then the white vapor poured from the

Stantler's antlers again. The vapor wafted down the street and passed over them.

Just then, as if they came out of nowhere, the Stantler herd appeared at the end of the street. The herd charged at the police station. Team Rocket ran off down the road.

"Everyone, into the station!" yelled Officer Jenny.

Ash ran toward the door. But he could see that Brock wasn't moving. His friend stood in the middle of the street — right in the path of the stampeding herd.

"Brock, what are you doing?" Ash called out.

"Trust me," Brock said. He held his hands out to the little Stantler, who stood a few feet away. "No need to be afraid. I won't hurt you."

"Brock, those Stantler are going to hurt you!" Misty cried.

Brock stood his ground. The Stantler ran closer and closer. Brock was a few feet away from being trampled.

"Brock!" Ash yelled. He ran out into the street.

Officer Jenny held him back. "It's too late, Ash."

Togepi covered its eyes. Ash couldn't bear to look, either. The herd was just inches away from Brock.

"Nooooo!" Ash screamed.

The stampeding herd charged, snorting and stomping, up to Brock. . . .

And then they passed right through him.

Ash gasped. It was as if the herd were made of air!

The last Stantler passed through Brock.

Then the entire herd vanished completely.

Brock let out a deep sigh. He turned to the others.

"See?" he said. "I told you there was nothing to worry about."

10

Giant Robot Stantler!

Ash shook his head. "I still can't believe you did that, Brock. You really scared us."

"*Pika!*" agreed Pikachu.

They were back at the police station. Brock was bandaging the wound on the little Stantler.

"You see, I figured out that the herd was just an illusion," Brock explained. "This young Stantler was creating the illusion to protect itself."

"That makes sense," Misty said.

"Stantler can produce illusions with the

round balls on its antlers," added Brock.

Ash turned to Officer Jenny. "Well, it looks like this mystery is solved."

"I must admit I'm impressed, Brock," said Officer Jenny. "How did you keep your cool?"

Brock blushed. "It was nothing. I saw the herd pass right through a building. That's when I figured that this little guy was behind it all."

The young Stantler was sleeping peacefully. Misty gentled stroked its head.

"This little Stantler sure has caused some big trouble," Misty said.

"It couldn't help it," Brock explained. "It was lost and alone in the park. It was scared. That's why it created the illusion of the herd to protect itself."

"Speaking of the herd," said Ash, "we should get this young Stantler back to its family right away."

Brock examined the bandaged leg. "I think it'll be okay after a good night's sleep. We can help it find its herd in the morning."

Officer Jenny gave them some blankets,

and Ash and the others fell asleep in the police station. Brock stayed by the Stantler's side all night. The next morning, they took a trail out of town. Officer Jenny said it led to the mountains where Stantler herds were found.

They followed the tree-lined trail all morning. Soon the trees gave way to rocky cliffs. The trail broke off and led up the mountainside.

Brock faced Stantler. "All right," he said. "This path leads back to the mountains. The rest is up to you."

The Stantler didn't move.

"It doesn't seem to want to go," Ash remarked.

"Can't it stay with us?" Misty asked. "It's so cute."

Brock sadly shook his head. "It belongs with its herd. It's too young to come with us."

Brock looked into the Stantler's eyes.

"Don't you understand? It's for your own good," Brock said.

The Stantler hung its head.

"Come on, get going!" Brock shouted. Ash knew that although Brock sounded angry, he didn't mean it. He had to get the Stantler to go, no matter what it took.

"Hurry up!" Brock yelled.

The Stantler looked at Brock, hurt. Then it turned around and trotted up the path.

Ash put his arm on Brock's shoulder. "You okay, Brock?"

Brock nodded. "It's the best way. Come on, let's go back to town."

Ash and his friends walked back down the trail in silence. They all felt sad about saying good-bye to Stantler.

Suddenly, Pikachu stopped. The little yellow Pokémon turned around. It pointed up to the sky.

Ash turned. Floating over the mountain was a hot-air balloon decorated with a Meowth face.

Team Rocket!

"Oh, no! The little Stantler!" Misty cried.

Brock was way ahead of them. Ash watched his friend speed like lightning back to the mountains.

Ash, Misty, and Pikachu took off after Brock. They ran up the mountain path.

Ash skidded to a stop. There, stomping down the mountain, was a giant robot Stantler. The robot had a silver body and blue lights in its eyes. A net dangled from the robot's mouth.

And inside the net was the little Stantler.

The Stantler kicked and struggled. White vapor came out of its antlers, covering the robot's head.

Up in the balloon, Team Rocket grinned triumphantly.

"Too bad," said James. "You can't fool a metal machine with illusions."

Brock ran up the mountain. He jumped up and tried to grab the net.

"Let it go!" Brock yelled. "This Stantler belongs in the wild, with its family."

Meowth held out a remote control.

"What can we do to make you see things our way?" Meowth wondered. "Oh, I know." The scratch cat Pokémon pressed a red button on the controls.

The robot's mouth opened, and metal rods shot out. The rods slammed into the ground all around Brock, trapping him.

"No!" Brock cried.

Jessie sneered. "Is that all you can say?" she said. "Not very creative, is it?"

"You really should get a good motto," James said. "Of course, ours is taken."

Brock knocked down the metal rods. Then he threw a red-and-white Poké Ball.

"Onix! Tackle!" Brock cried.

Light flashed, and out came a Pokémon that looked like a snake made of huge gray rocks. Ash knew that Onix was probably

Brock's most powerful Pokémon.

Onix didn't hesitate. The Pokémon slammed into the robot Stantler. The robot rocked back and forth.

"Onix, Bind Attack!" commanded Brock.

Onix wrapped its long body around the robot Stantler, squeezing the metal. There was a sickening sound as the robot collapsed under the incredible pressure.

Onix released its grip. The robot

exploded in a mess of wires and gears.

"*Ohhhhhhhhhhhh!*" roared Onix in a gravelly voice.

"Good work, Onix!" Brock cheered.

Ash started to cheer, too. Then he noticed something.

A net dangled from the basket of Team Rocket's balloon.

"Brock!" Ash shouted. "They've still got the Stantler!"

86

11

Save That Stantler!

The balloon rose into the air.

"*Nyah nyah nyah nyah nyah,*" taunted James. "You can't get us!"

Ash thought fast. "Pikachu, Thunderbolt!" he told the Electric Pokémon.

"*Pikachuuuuuu!*" The air sizzled as Pikachu hurled a bolt of electricity at the balloon.

But the attack fell short.

"Your puny Pikachu attack can't reach us!" said Meowth gleefully. "We're too high!"

Ash quickly threw another Poké Ball. He

wasn't going to let Team Rocket get away.

"Bulbasaur, use your Vine Whip. Fast!" Ash yelled.

Bulbasaur appeared and quickly jumped up on a high rock. Long green vines lashed out of its plant bulb.

The vines couldn't reach. The balloon floated away, over the treetops.

"No!" Brock cried.

Jessie and James rolled their eyes. "He really does need a better line than that," Jessie said.

Suddenly, a loud rumbling echoed across the mountains. Ash watched, amazed, as a large herd of Stantler gathered on a cliff just above them.

"Is that an illusion, too?" Misty asked.

Brock shook his head. "I don't think so. I think they're here to help."

The largest Stantler in the herd took a flying leap off the cliff. The Stantler soared through the sky, ripping the net with its antlers. It also tore a hole in Team Rocket's balloon.

"Looks like Team Rocket's running away

again!" Ash said, as Jessie, James, and Meowth ran out of the fallen balloon and into the woods.

Ash turned to Brock. "We did it. We saved the Stantler!"

Bulbasaur set the young Stantler on the ground. The Stantler herd came out of the woods, led by the large Stantler. It nuzzled the Stantler's nose.

"See," Brock said softly. "I told you this is where you belong."

The young Stantler looked into Brock's eyes. Then it turned around and followed the herd.

"Good luck, little guy," Brock whispered as the Stantler herd disappeared around a bend.

Misty leaned back against a tall tree. "That was something," she remarked. "This city looked like such a peaceful place. But I'm exhausted from all this action!"

"It certainly is interesting out here in the west," Brock said. "I wonder what's waiting for us in Violet Town?"

Ash grinned. "It's a mystery to me!"

POKéMON

GOTTA READ 'EM ALL!™